Fun In The Sun

Written by Ski Michaels
Illustrated by Diane Paterson

Troll Associates

Library of Congress Cataloging in Publication Data

———

Fun in the sun.

Summary: Billy Beaver cannot persuade his animal
friends to play in the sun until he tempts them with
the prospect of swimming at his new dam.
  [1. Play—Fiction. 2. Swimming—Fiction.
3. Beavers—Fiction. 4. Animals—Fiction]
I. Paterson, Diane, 1946-   ill.   II. Title.
PZ7.P3656Fu   1986   [E]   85-14055
ISBN 0-8167-0568-2 (lib. bdg.)
ISBN 0-8167-0569-0 (pbk.)

Fun In The Sun

Up went the sun. It was a hot
sun. It was a hot day. It was a
hot, sunny day.

Billy Beaver got up. He looked
out.
"What a sunny day!" said Billy.
"What a good day to play."

Billy Beaver went out.
"I will have fun in the sun," said
Billy.

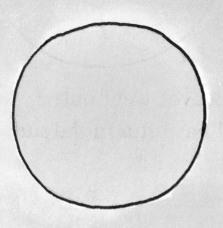

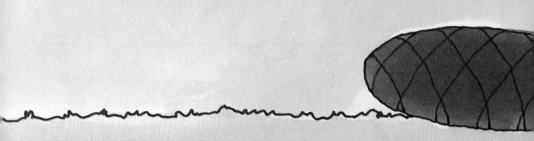

Did Billy have fun? No! He
wanted to play. But there was no
one to play with.

The sun was hot—it was too, too hot. No one was playing out in the sun.

"This is not fun," said Billy. "I want someone to play with."

Billy went to see Mandy Mouse.
Mandy Mouse was fun to play
with. Would Mandy play with
Billy Beaver?

Mandy Mouse was sitting in the
shade of a big tree.
"Do you want to play?" said
Billy. "It will be fun to play in
the sun."

"Oh no!" said Mandy. "The sun is too hot today. The shade is cool. I do not want to play."

Away went Billy Beaver. He
went to look for someone else to
play with.

Billy went to see Fred Fox. Fred
Fox was fun to play with. Was it
too hot for Fred to play?
"Will you play today?" said Billy
Beaver. "It is sunny. We can
have fun."

Fred Fox was having a drink of
cool water.

"What?" cried Fred. "Play
today? It is too hot! I do not
want to play. I would rather
have some cool water."

"There is cool water in the brook," said Billy. "We can play in the water. We can swim in the water. We can play and swim. Swimming is fun."

16

"Swimming is fun," said Fred.
"But we cannot swim in the
brook. The brook's water is cool,
but it is not deep enough to swim
in."

Away went Billy Beaver. What a day! It was sunny and no one would play. Mandy Mouse would not play. Fred Fox would not play. Was it that hot?

Billy went to see Ron Raccoon.
Ron liked to play. Would Ron
Raccoon play on this hot day?

Ron Raccoon was making a fan.
A fan is good to have on a hot
day.

"Do you want to play?" said
Billy. "The sun is up. We can
have fun."

Ron did not want to play.
"Do you want to make a fan?"
he asked Billy. "I can fan you.
You can fan me. We can be cool
on a hot, sunny day."

"No," said Billy Beaver. "I do
not like to make fans."
Ron said, "What do beavers like
to make?"

"Beavers like to make dams,"
said Billy.
Billy stopped.
"A beaver dam!" he cried. "I
must go!"

"Wait!" cried Ron Raccoon.
"What are you going to do?"
But Billy Beaver did not hear
him. Away went Billy.

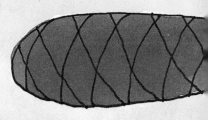

Billy Beaver went to the brook.
What a good place for a beaver
dam!

Billy looked at the brook.
"A beaver dam will stop the
water," he said. "The cool water
will get deep. It will be a good
place to swim."

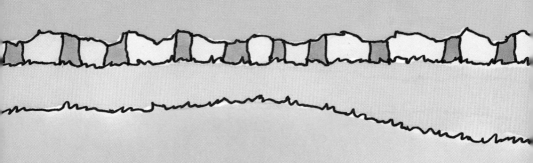

Billy looked up at the sun.
"It is too hot to play," he said.
"But it is not too hot to make a
beaver dam."

Billy went to work. The beaver dam went up. Billy's dam stopped the cool brook water.

The water got deeper and
deeper. What a good beaver
dam it was! What a good place
to swim!

"I want to have fun in the sun,"
said Billy. "Will someone swim
with me?"

Billy Beaver went to see Mandy
Mouse.
"I made a beaver dam," he said.
"We can get cool in the water.
We can have fun."

Mandy got up out of the shade.
"I want to have fun in the sun,"
she cried. "I will go swiming."

Billy went to see Fred Fox.
"I stopped up the brook," said
Billy. "The water is cool and
deep. We can swim in it."

34

"Yea!" cried Fred. "I want to
play. I will swim with you."

Billy went to see Ron Raccoon.
"Do you want to make fans?" he
said. "Or do you want to swim?"

"I want to swim!" cried Ron
Raccoon.

Mandy Mouse went to the brook.

Fred Fox went to the brook.

Ron Raccoon went to the brook.

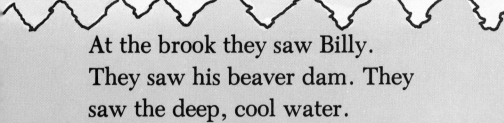

At the brook they saw Billy.
They saw his beaver dam. They
saw the deep, cool water.

"What a good place to swim," cried Fred.

Billy looked at Mandy Mouse.
He looked at Fred Fox and Ron
Raccoon.
"Into the water!" he shouted.

And into the brook they went!

The water was cool. The sun did
not feel too hot anymore.

"A sunny day is fun," said
Mandy.

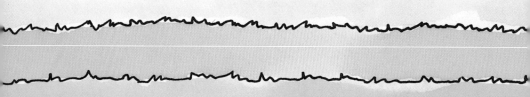

"Swimming is fun," said Fred
Fox.

"Billy Beaver is fun," said Ron
Raccoon. "He knows how to play
on a hot, sunny day!"